ENTER the PENGUIN

Steve Barlow · Steve Skidmore

Illustrated by Lee Robinson

Franklin Watts
First published in Great Britain in 2018
by The Watts Publishing Group

Text © Steve Barlow and Steve Skidmore 2018
Illustrations © The Watts Publishing Group 2018
Illustrator: Lee Robinson
Design: Cathryn Gilbert
Editor: Katie Woolley

ISBN 978 1 4451 5924 9
ebook ISBN 978 1 4451 5925 6
Library ebook ISBN 978 1 4451 5926 3

1 3 5 7 9 10 8 6 4 2

Printed in Great Britain

MIX
Paper from
responsible sources
FSC® C104740

Franklin Watts
An imprint of
Hachette Children's Group
Part of The Watts Publishing Group
Carmelite House
50 Victoria Embankment
London EC4Y 0DZ

An Hachette UK Company
www.hachette.co.uk

www.franklinwatts.co.uk

HOW TO BE A HERO

With most books, you read from the beginning to the end and then stop. You can then read it backwards if you like, but that would be silly.

But in this book, you're the hero. That's why it's called *I Hero*, see?

You read a bit, then you make a choice that takes you to a different part of the book. You might jump from Section 3 to Section 47 or Section 28. Crazy, huh?

If you make a good choice, **GREAT!**

BUUUUUUT...

If you make the wrong choice, **ALL KINDS OF BAD STUFF WILL HAPPEN.**

Hah-ha! Loser! You'll have to start again.

But that won't happen to you, will it?
Because you're not a zero — **YOU'RE A HERO!**

THIS IS YOU!

You are a **ninja penguin**. Cool hey! That's because you were born in the Antarctic and it's **VERY COLD** there!

But years ago, you left home to train with the great shinobi masters of Japan. They taught you **AWESOME** ninja skills!

Now you wander the world, a flipper for hire. But you never forget that your true calling is to right wrongs and help those who cannot help themselves.

You know that you will only succeed when you follow **the Way of the Penguin**.

The Way Of The Penguin Ninja

- YOU work in secret, and only fight openly when YOU must.

- YOU are an expert in disguise, deception and trickery.

- YOU turn your enemies' strength against them.

- YOU will do anything for a bucket of fish.

Go to 1.

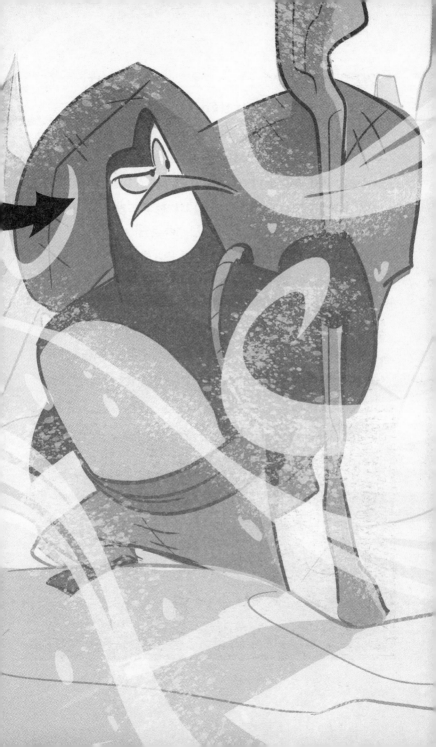

1

As you travel on foot through the lands of the **Arctic Circle**, you arrive at a seal village where you are hoping to rest for the night.

But the village has been invaded by three walruses who are throwing their weight about, terrifying the seals.

"Get out of here, stranger," a fleeing seal tells you. "Daddy Bear has sent his heavies to steal our fish harvest."

You know that Daddy Bear is the leader of a **gang of bandits**. They really are bad news bears. Should you interfere or not? You consider **the Way of the Penguin**.

If you decide the seals' troubles are not your problem, go to 13.

If you decide to stick your beak in, go to 27.

2

You divide the seals into squads. You, Foxy, Jagger, Snowy and Bigfoot train a squad each.

"Shouldn't we be building defences?" asks Foxy.

"And keeping a lookout?" adds Snowy.

"Don't worry," you say. "I know what I'm doing."

Go to 20.

3

You leap through the window and join the fight, your flippers delivering powerful **ninja** kicks and chops. Soon, wolves are flying left and right.

WHAM! CRUNCH!

"Thanks, partner!" cries Foxy as you send a wolf sailing over your head to land on the honky-tonk piano. It collapses with a jangle of broken strings.

But the wolves are **fighting mad**, and no matter how many you lay out, more keep coming.

Go to 35.

4

"Charge!" you cry.

Leading Foxy, Jagger and Bigfoot into the fray, you head straight for Daddy Bear. But your eagerness is your undoing. You are temporarily blinded by a snowball bursting nearby. You wipe snow from your eyes — but you are too late. The great bear's gigantic paw crushes you into the snow. You've been put on ice!

You have forgotten the Way of the Penguin — only fight when you must! Go back to 1.

5

"Those walruses won't be back in a hurry," you tell the villagers.

"Maybe not," says the head seal, "but Daddy Bear will be **angry** that you have defied him, and when he brings his gang here we shall all suffer..."

To seek help to protect the village, go to 31.

To try and reason with Daddy Bear, go to 18.

"Hold firm," you tell the seals, "and trust me."

You stand on the ice wall and look out. Snowy is right. The bears are out on the sea-ice, and homing in on the village.

To take on the bears single-flippered, go to 12.

To trick the bears, go to 26.

7

"I am sorry they tried to cheat you," you tell the wolves, "but I need them. Let them go."

The wolves are **angry**. "You don't tell us what to do!" growls the leader.

The wolves spring!

Go to 35.

8

You take shelter in a snow cave. While they are chilling, you tell your old comrades about Daddy Bear and the seals.

"Sounds dangerous," says Foxy. "What's in it for us?"

"**Who cares**," snarls Jagger, "as long as there's fighting? Lemme at 'em!"

You hold up a flipper. Your sensitive **ninja** hearing has picked up faint footsteps.

"Wait! There's someone outside."

The wolverine rushes out of the cave. There is a **scuffle** and a moment later he reappears, dragging in a snowshoe hare.

"Who are you?" you ask. "And what do you want?"

"Name's Bigfoot," says the hare defiantly. "I saw how you tricked those wolves. I want to help you **whup** those bears."

To let the hare join you, go to 19.
To turn down the offer, go to 30.
To see how well Bigfoot can fight, go to 40.

9

As you head for the village, you realise that you are being followed.

"Don't look now," says Foxy, "but I think we have a bear on our tail."

You smile. "No. It is Bigfoot following us. My highly-tuned ninja hearing tells me so. Plus, I just saw him dodge behind a snowdrift."

Jagger growls. "You want me to tear him to pieces a little?"

To order Jagger to attack Bigfoot, go to 21.

If you'd rather he let Bigfoot be, go to 36.

10

You gather everyone together.

"I will teach you the Way of the Penguin," you say. "First you must practise meditation."

You make all the seals sit in the lotus position, close their eyes and chant, "Ommmm…"

"This is a waste of time," protests Bigfoot.

"Silence!" you say. "You're disturbing the karma."

Bigfoot scowls. "I karma help feeling we're sitting ducks…"

Go to 20.

You head towards the noise. Before long, a snowy owl appears. It dives at a snowdrift, only to pull away with empty talons. "**Aw, strewth!**"

You laugh. "Well, if it isn't my old friend Snowy. What are you doing here?"

The great bird peers at you short-sightedly. "That you, **Penguin**? I'm trying to catch some supper, but those voles and lemmings are fast little bludgers and my eyesight isn't what it was. I can see them well enough from the air, but when I pounce they are **gone**!"

If you want Snowy to join your team, go to 44.

If you don't want to drag him into this fight, go to 41.

If you are disappointed that Snowy is too blind to fight, go to 17.

12

You step out onto the ice. As the bears approach, you hold up a flipper.

"**Halt!**" you cry. "This village is well defended! Leave now!" The bears laugh. "Alright," you say, "you asked for it."

You rush to the attack. The bears beat you into a slush-penguin.

You think a penguin can take on an army of polar bears? **THE ANSWER IS NO!** Go back to 1.

13

The unhappy villagers hand their fish over to the walruses.

When they have gone, you ask the head seal if you can get supper and somewhere to stay.

"Supper?" he honks. "The walruses took our supper — and you did nothing to help! You won't find a welcome here!"

What kind of a ninja are you? Go back to 1.

14

"What's going on here?" you cry.

The wolf pack leader turns on you with a snarl. **"Stay out of this, fishface."**

You bow. "I regret I am unable to comply, wolf-san."

The wolf looks puzzled. "Say what?"

"I said, '**No, dogbreath.**'"

The wolf snarls. "I'll get you for that!"

To attack the wolf, go to 43.
To talk to the wolves, go to 25.

15

You arrive back at the seal village, but it seems deserted. Frightened eyes peer out of doorways. The villagers are hiding!

"**Come out!**" you call.

The head seal approaches you in a flap.

"Go away!" he honks. "You will only bring us trouble. We're leaving the village!"

"**You cowards!**"

You turn round to see who has spoken, and realise that it is Bigfoot.

To let Bigfoot speak, go to 22.

To argue with the seals yourself, go to 42.

To let the seals leave, go to 37.

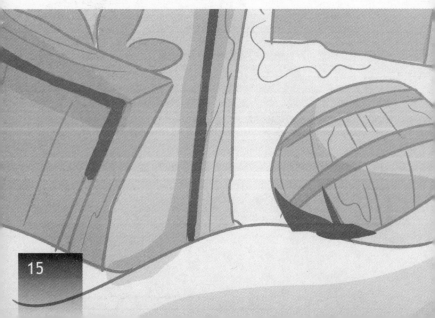

16

"Don't let them get away!" you cry.

When the bears reach the sea, they turn and fight. Leading the charge, you see many seals fall to the bears' mighty paws before a **terrible blow** sends you tumbling into the sea — where leopard seals are waiting for a quick penguin snack!

Go back to 1.

17

You scowl at your old friend. "You used to be a fighter." You laugh bitterly. "Look at you now! **Blind as a bat...**"

You have already turned away when Snowy swoops down and carries you away in his talons.

"My eyes might not be any good for spotting voles," he squawks, "but they're plenty good enough to p-p-p-pick up a pesky penguin."

"Put me down!" you yell.

"Whatever you say!" Snowy laughs and lets go.

"HEEEEELLLLLPPPPPPP!"

You fall from the air screaming, and splatter like a dropped ice cream.

Rude is never funny. Go back to 1.

You go and find the bears, asking to be taken to their leader.

"Now look here," you tell Daddy Bear, "you're being absolutely beastly to those poor seals. I want to you shake paws — er, flippers — whatever, and be friends."

Daddy Bear signals to his bodyguards, who beat you to a **jelly**.

Whatever happened to secrecy? Not to mention common sense! Go back to 1.

"Sure," you say, "the more the merrier."

"Wait a minute!" snaps Foxy. "Jagger and I are professionals. We're not teaming up with any old **chucklehead**."

They head out into the blizzard. While you are trying to decide whether to go after them, a polar bear sticks its muzzle into your cave.

"Comfortable?" he asks. "**You won't be**." He raises his voice. "Stamp away up there!"

The snow around you trembles. The bears are stamping on the roof of the cave. Before you can act, **the snow caves in**.

It's **snow joke**! You are buried alive! Go back to 1.

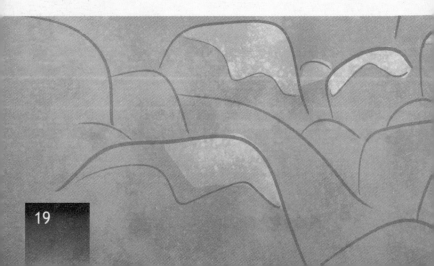

20

Unfortunately, you are totally unprepared when Daddy Bear's gang mounts a sneak attack.

SPLAT! CRUNCH! THUNK!

The seals drop their makeshift weapons and waddle for their lives. The bears steal the fish and destroy the village.

You've been caught cold.

Go back to 1.

21

"We don't want him," you say. "Teach him a lesson."

Foxy and Jagger turn round and rush to the attack. But Bigfoot puts up an unexpectedly stiff fight, and the battle is making a lot of noise.

ZAP!

THWAAAM!

KAPOW!

"**Stop!**" you cry. "The bears will hear you! We must get away from here!"

Leaving Bigfoot behind, you go on your way. Go to 49.

22

"We're not all **ninjas**," protests the head seal.

"I'm not a **ninja** either," snaps Bigfoot, "but I'm here because I'm not afraid to fight in a good cause. You should be fighting for your homes, for your people, for your livelihood. I'm fighting because those bears have no right to treat you this way. I don't even like fish!"

The seals look sheepish.

"Your courage shames us," says the head seal. "We will fight. Tell us what to do."

To set to work building defences, go to 34.
To train all the seals to fight, go to 2.

23

Your stand calmly as the walruses pound towards you. At the last possible moment, you step aside and the powerful creatures bang their heads together...

RACK!!!

You bow to your vanquished foes.

"In the immortal words of a great ninja master, '**Hit the road, sleazebags!**'"

The dazed creatures slither away, swearing revenge.

You expect the seals to be happy that you have driven off their enemies, but instead they are very worried.

"Daddy Bear isn't going to like this," moans their leader.

Go to 5.

Foxy has escaped from his guard. With the bears on the back paw, you send him, Jagger and Bigfoot into the fray.

THWACK! BASH! WALLOP!

Snowy flies at the bears' heads. "These bludgers are a bigger target than lemmings!" he hoots.

But his excitement is his undoing! Daddy Bear swats Snowy out of the sky.

"Surrender," he growls, "or the owl gets it!"

To order the seals to carry on fighting, go to 45.

To challenge Daddy Bear to single combat, go to 32.

25

You hold up a flipper in a peaceful gesture.

"I only wanted to ask why you are fighting."

The wolf pack leader glares at Foxy and Jagger. "We caught them cheating at cards."

Foxy shrugs. "A minor misunderstanding."

"You had fifty-two aces up your sleeve!" howls the pack leader.

You glare at Foxy.

"Okay, maybe not so minor," he admits.

To order the wolves to let Foxy and Jagger go, go to 7.

To agree that they should be punished, go to 47.

26

You tell the villagers to hide. Then you watch as Foxy appears, limping, near the bears and allows himself to be captured by them.

"They got my buddy!" roars Jagger. "I'll pulverise 'em!"

"Calm down," you tell the wolverine. "It's all part of my plan."

Snowy, who has been flying silently above the bears, comes in to land.

"Your plan's working, mate!" he reports. "Foxy's told the bears he was running away because all the seals have scarpered."

You nod. "When the bears get here, they'll be off their guard."

To stop the bears before they reach the village, go to 48.

To allow the bears into the village, go to 39.

27

You step in front of the walrus enforcers and bow.

"Honourable whiskery ones," you begin...

The walruses aren't in any mood to listen to you.

"Get lost, shorty!" one growls.

If you want to reason with the walruses, go to 33.

If you want to attack them, go to 46.

Your journey onwards leads you into an ice canyon.

As you go round a bend of the canyon, you hear sounds echoing from its walls — growls, and creaks of breaking ice. Angry polar bears appear along the lip of the canyon. You have walked into Daddy Bear's ambush.

RUUUUUMBLE!

An avalanche of snow and ice, started by the bears, roars down upon you. In seconds you are buried alive.

A ninja should never walk blindly into the unknown! Go back to 1.

29

You and Bigfoot have taught the seals to use their strengths against the bears.

Foxy reports that the defences are completed. "We've dug a moat, and we're keeping it clear of ice," he says, "and we've built an ice wall around the village. We've even set up that ramp you wanted, but I can't imagine what it's for."

"You'll see," you tell him.

Snowy comes in to land. "The bears are coming!" he squawks. "They mean business."

The seals panic! "This is unbearable!" cries their leader. "We can't fight them. We must get away!"

To let the seals go, turn to 37.
To rally the seals, go to 6.

30

"Sorry," you say, "there's no room for amateurs on this team."

"Who are you calling an amateur?" demands Bigfoot. "What's an amateur, anyway?"

You stick your beak out of the cave. "The snow's stopped." You turn to Foxy and Jagger. "Well? Are you coming?"

Foxy shrugs. "We don't have anything else to do."

You leave the cave and start to lead the way towards the village.

Go to 9.

31

"Even with my help," you say, "you cannot protect your village. Daddy Bear's gang is too strong. But I will find others to come to your aid."

You leave the frightened seals and make your way to **Klancy's Klondike Saloon**, a tavern where hunters, trappers and such riff-raff gather. Snow is falling as you arrive, and a look at the sky tells you that there will soon be a storm.

A fight is going on inside the saloon. A wolf bursts through a window and lands in the snow at your feet.

You look through the broken window. Inside, you see that a fox and a wolverine are fighting off a whole pack of wolves. These are Foxy and Jagger, the old comrades you have come here to find.

THWACK!
POW!
BAM!

To join in with the fight against the wolves, go to 3.

To find out what the fight is about, go to 14.

"Let's settle this now, bear to penguin!" you tell Daddy Bear. "I challenge you!"

The great bear roars, and surges forward to attack. Bears and seals stop fighting to watch the battle, open-mouthed.

Daddy Bear is powerful, but slow. You are fast and agile. Even so, the bear lands a cuff that sends you flying through the air.

Foxy groans. "He's going to be filleted!"

"No! Look!" Jagger points.

You have invited Daddy Bear's blow, riding his punch to set up your master move — the Penguin Slide. You land at the top of the snow ramp you had the seals build. You slither down it on your belly, and slam into the bear chief with the speed of a rocket, using your feet and flippers to devastating effect.

SMACK! FLAPLAPALAP!
THOOM!

Seeing their leader fall, the terrified bears flee.

To order an attack on the bears, go to 16.
To let the bears go, go to 50.

33

You bow again. "I am sure we can come to some reasonable agreement..."

The walruses sneer at you. "You want a fight, titch? Put your flippers where your beak is!"

You decide that these creatures are not open to reason.

"Okay, flabby!" you squawk. "You asked for it!"

Go to 46.

34

You order Foxy and Jagger to organise defences while you and Bigfoot train the seals and Snowy flies above looking for danger. You have to decide the best way to prepare the seals to fight.

To train the seals in the Way of the Penguin, go to 10.

To teach the seals simple self-defence, go to 29.

35

Busily fighting off snarling wolves who would like to wolf you down in a jiffy, you fail to notice the musk ox bartender creeping up behind you. He is carrying a heavy wooden bench, which he swings with enormous strength.

THWACK!

The bench smacks into your skull, and you briefly see starfish before slumping to the floor, out for the count.

You've forgotten the Way of the Penguin. You should use deception and trickery, only fighting when you must! Go back to 1.

You smile. "Never mind. Let him alone. If he's strong enough to follow us, he may be useful after all."

Your path leads you to the foot of some ice-mountains. From the valley up ahead, you hear angry squawks and *THUMPS*. A bad-tempered voice calls, "Come here, yer little perisher! I got yer! Where are yer? Stay still, ya mongrel!"

"What's that?" asks Foxy.

"I don't know," you say, "but it sounds like trouble."

If you want to find out what the noise is all about, go to 11.

To avoid trouble by going another way, go to 49.

37

"Run away if you must!" you cry. "We'll protect your village alone!"

By the time the bears attack, the seals have gone. Without them, your small team is no match for **Daddy Bear's gang**.

Go back to 1.

38

You attack one of the walruses, but his blubbery hide absorbs your blows while the other jumps you from behind. You lie winded while both walruses take it in turns to bounce their gigantic bodies up and down on you, squashing you against the ice until you are a penguin pizza.

SPLAT!

You have forgotten the Way of the Penguin. You must use your enemies' strength against them! Go back to 1.

39

Daddy Bear leads his forces into the village. They are relaxed, already celebrating an easy victory...

"Attack!" you cry.

The seals you have ordered to hide under the snow suddenly rise up at the bears' feet, bowling them over and flinging them skywards with their powerful tails. Under your direction, more seals emerge from their igloos. Some lift *GIGANTIC* pre-prepared snowballs on their noses and throw them up for leaping seals to spike with their flippers, hitting the astonished bears in the face with great accuracy.

To join the fight, go to 4.
To stay back and direct the defence,
go to 24.

"Very well," you say, "show us what you can do."

"You got it!" says Bigfoot eagerly. He heads out of the cave.

The storm has passed. Bigfoot points to a snow-covered tree.

"Watch this!" He launches a flying drop-kick at the tree with his **massive** snowshoe feet.

BA-DOOOOING!

The tree bends under Bigfoot's attack, then springs back, slamming him into the ground. He tries to get up, but falls back unconscious.

"Nice move!" says Foxy. He turns to you. "You want this **loser** on the team?"

You shake your head, and turn towards the seal village with Foxy and Jagger following.

Go to 9.

41

"Where yer goin'?" asks Snowy. "Can I help? I could be yer eye in the sky."

You shake your head. "Thanks, but no thanks."

You say goodbye to Snowy and carry on. But without the owl spotting for you, you have no warning of what's ahead...

Go to 28.

42

"He's right!" you cry. "Call yourselves seals? You're nothing but jellyfish!"

The seals are **angry**, and Jagger is already spoiling for a fight. As the argument becomes a brawl, you realise that you risk hurting the people you were supposed to save, especially when during the fight their precious fish are scattered and stolen by gulls and skuas.

You are no better than the bears!
Go back to 1.

43

You perform a **Leaping Tiger** kick that sends the wolf flying through the air. It crashes into a table, reducing it to matchwood, before slumping unconscious to the ground.

CRAAAASH!

But the other wolves close in on you, **snarling** ferociously. They leap to the attack.

Go to 35.

44

You tell Snowy of your mission. "Will you join us?"

"Hold on!" cries Foxy. "How is a blind old owl going to help us?"

"Who says I'm blind, yer ratbag?" hoots the owl angrily. "I still see fair dinkum over a distance. I can be yer eye in the sky."

Snowy takes off and circles overhead before landing at your feet.

"Don't go down the canyon up ahead," he says, "unless yer want be dry-gulched by polar bears. And yer got a hare following yer."

"I know," you tell him. "Welcome to the team."

Go to 15.

"**Attack!**" you cry.

The seals are horrified. Their leader throws his harpoon down at your feet. "You don't care what happens to your friend?" he cries. "You're worse than the bears!"

All around you, the demoralised seals are surrendering.

A true ninja does not abandon a friend! Go back to 1.

You attack the nearest walrus with an **Iron Flipper** punch, knocking one of his tusks out.

CHOP!!!!

The other two walruses are **angry**.

"Let's get him," one growls as they charge towards you.

To attack the walruses, go to 38.

If you would rather let them attack you, go to 23.

"If they were cheating," you tell the wolves, "they must be punished. I will help you take them to the jail."

By the time you leave the saloon, the snowstorm is raging. The wolves are instantly blinded by the driving snow.

"Now!" you tell Foxy and Jagger. "Run!"

Within moments, you have lost the wolves. You know that the snow will cover your tracks and destroy your scent. Behind you, the wolves howl in frustration.

Go to 8.

"**Charge!**" you cry.

The seals emerge from hiding. They pour out of the village and attack the bears.

But their bravery is no match for the bears' strength and experience. You haven't helped the seals — you have only sealed their fate!

You have forgotten the Way of the Penguin! What happened to disguise and deception? Go back to 1.

You hurry Foxy and Jagger along, but as you cross a frozen inlet where great slabs of ice have been thrown up by the sea, you hear furtive noises all around you. You stop to listen — and Daddy Bear and his **gang** appear from behind the shattered blocks of ice. They have you surrounded, and outnumbered.

"**Hello, punk,**" growls Daddy Bear. "Do you know why polar bears don't eat **penguins**?"

"No," you say.

"No reason," says Daddy Bear. He turns to his gang. "**Get him!**"

You go down fighting. But the important thing is, you go down.

You have walked into a trap. You have forgotten the Way of the Penguin!
Go back to 1.

"Let them go," you tell the seals. "They won't
be back."

The seals are delighted that you have saved
their village and driven Daddy Bear's gang away.
They offer you a reward.

"I seek no reward," you say. "On the other
flipper, if you have a **bucket of fish to
spare...?**"

They bring you some fish they had managed to
stash away from Daddy Bear and the hungry gulls.
They offer it to you and invite you to stay.

"Thank you," you say, "but our destiny lies
elsewhere."

You gather your
team and prepare to
move on to wherever
your help may be
needed. For that is the
ninja code; that is

**the Way
of
the
Penguin**.

I HERO
TOONS
KiLLER CUSTARD
EDGE
Steve Barlow · Steve Skidmore
Illustrated by Lee Robinson

We all know that school can be boring sometimes...same old teachers, same old lessons, same old routine.

I bet you wish that just occasionally something exciting would happen.

But there's an old saying, "Be careful what you wish for." Today is about to get *INTERESTING*...

1

It is lunchtime at your school. You are queueing up and see that there is a new cook behind the counter.

"What's for pudding?" you ask.

"Apple pie," the new cook replies. "What do you want with it? Ice cream, **or my very special custard?**"

To choose the ice cream, go to 25.

To choose the special custard, go to 45.

Continue the adventure in:

About the 2Steves

"The 2Steves" are
Britain's most popular
writing double act
for young people,
specialising in comedy
and adventure. They
perform regularly in schools and libraries,
and at festivals, taking the power of words
and story to audiences of all ages.

Together they have written many books,
including the *I HERO Immortals* and *iHorror* series.

About the illustrator: Lee Robinson

Lee studied animation at Newcastle College and
went on to work on comics such as *Kung Fu
Panda* as well as running comicbook workshops
throughtout the northeast of England. When he's not
drawing, Lee loves running, reading and videogames.
He now lives in Edmonton, Canada, where's he's got
plenty of time to come up with crazy ideas while
waiting for the weather to warm up.

I HERO Legends — collect them all!

ATHENA
978 1 4451 5234 9 pb
978 1 4451 5235 6 ebook

BEOWULF
978 1 4451 5225 7 pb
978 1 4451 5226 4 ebook

KING ARTHUR
978 1 4451 5231 8 pb
978 1 4451 5232 5 ebook

FREYA
978 1 4451 5237 0 pb
978 1 4451 5238 7 ebook

HERCULES
978 1 4451 5228 8 pb
978 1 4451 5229 5 ebook

ROBIN HOOD
978 1 4451 5183 0 pb
978 1 4451 5184 7 ebook

Have you read the I HERO Monster Hunter series?

ALIEN
978 1 4451 5878 5 pb
978 1 4451 5876 1 ebook

GHOST
978 1 4451 5939 3 pb
978 1 4451 5940 9 ebook

MUTANT
978 1 4451 5945 4 pb
978 14451 5946 1 ebook

VAMPIRE
978 1 4451 5936 2 pb
978 1 4451 5937 9 ebook

WEREWOLF
978 1 4451 5942 3 pb
978 1 4451 5943 0 ebook

ZOMBIE
978 1 4451 5935 5 pb
978 1 4451 5933 1 ebook

Also by the 2Steves...

978 1 4451 5104 5 pb
978 1 4451 5119 9 eBook

You are a skilled, stealthy ninja.
Your village has been attacked by a
warlord called Raiden. Now YOU must
go to his castle and stop him before
he destroys more lives.

978 1 4451 5101 4 pb
978 1 4451 5117 5 eBook

You are the Warrior Princess.
Someone wants to steal the magical
ice diamonds from the Crystal
Caverns. YOU must discover who
it is and save your kingdom.

978 1 4451 5103 8 pb
978 1 4451 5121 2 eBook

You are a magical unicorn.
Empress Yin Yang has stolen Carmine,
the red unicorn. Yin Yang wants to
destroy the colourful Rainbow Land.
YOU must stop her!

978 1 4451 5102 1 pb
978 1 4451 5124 3 eBook

You are a spy, codenamed Scorpio.
Someone has taken control of secret
satellite laser weapons. YOU must find
out who is responsible and
stop their dastardly plans.